FUNNY
TRAIL TALES

edited by

Amy Kelley

FA

Cover illustrations by Peter Grosshauser.

Text illustrations by Amy Kelley unless otherwise noted.

Grateful acknowledgment is made to those who granted permission to reprint the selections in this book. A complete list of copyright permissions is found on the following two pages.

Cataloging-in-Publication Data is on record at the Library of Congress.

Acknowledgments

"Camping" from *Dave Barry's Only Travel guide You'll Ever Need* by Dave Barry. Copyright © 1991 by Dave Barry Reprinted by permission of Ballantine Books, a division of Random House Inc.

Illustration from *Dave Barry's Only Travel guide You'll Ever Need* by Patrick O'Brien. Illustrations copyright © 1991 by Random House Inc. Reprinted by permission of Ballantine Books, a division of Random House Inc.

"Bad Advice," from *Jaguars Ripped My Flesh*, by Tim Cahill. Copyright © 1987 by Tim Cahill. Reprinted with permission from Lowenstein Associates, Inc., New York.

Chapter 4 "Visiting Mrs. Murphy" from *Cheaper by the Dozen* by Frank B. Gilbreth, Jr. Copyright © 1948, 1963 by Frank B. Gilbreth Jr. and Ernestine Gilbreth Carey. Reprinted by permission of HarperCollins Publishers, Inc.

"Winter" from *Lake Wobegon Days* by Garrison Keilor. Copyright © 1985 by Garrison Keilor. Used by permission of Viking Penguin, a division of Penguin Putnam Inc.

"Get Lost" from *The Grasshopper Trap* by Patrick F. McManus. Copyright © 1985 by Patrick F. McManus. Reprinted by permission of Henry Holt and Company, LLC.

Contents

Introduction

I like to think of myself as someone who enjoys a good joke, although I can never remember them. And, I definitely love to laugh. When I took on this project—compiling a collection of short, humorous pieces about the outdoors—I thought it would be the perfect complement to the challenges I then faced at art school. Tim Cahill immediately came to mind as "poster child" for the type of writing I'd seek; I thought the toughest task would be selecting which pieces would be most universally acknowledged as funny.

As it turned out, finding humorous pieces that are also about the outdoors was more of a challenge than I'd anticipated. (You may notice in glancing through this book that I have taken some liberties .... Thank you Erin Turner and Peggy O'Neill-McLeod at Falcon for giving me some help and perspective in that department.)

That said, I hope that some of these pieces bring a smile to your face if you read them quietly, or a shared laugh if you read them aloud—and I do hope you read them aloud, because I chose these pieces with that in mind.

Camping brings out the kid in me: the sense of adventure, the eyes wide open listening to the "scary sounds" of the night woods, the having to go to the bathroom after I've taken off my boots and crawled into my sleeping bag… And so, some of these pieces are kid stories. Like Winne-the-Pooh, which actually was read aloud to me on a float trip. I loved it then, and still do.

They say that humor is the best medicine. Or maybe it's spending time outdoors that's the best medicine. Either way, if you're camping and you brought this book along, I hope you find you're in pretty good shape.

Enjoy.

Amy Kelley
May 1, 2000

Dave Barry

From "Camping" in *Dave Barry's Only Travel Guide You'll Ever Need*

Camping:
Nature's Way of Promoting the Motel Business

So far we've discussed many exciting travel destinations, but all of them lack an element that is too often missing from the stressful, high-pressure urban environment most of us live in. That element is: dirt. Also missing from the urban environment are snakes, pit toilets, and tiny black flies that crawl up your nose. To experience these things, you need to locate some Nature and go camping in it.

Where Nature is Located

Nature is located mainly in national parks, which are vast tracts of wilderness that have been set aside by the United States government so citizens will always have someplace to go where they can be attacked by bears. And we're not talking about ordinary civilian bears, either: We're talking about *federal* bears,. which can behave however they want to because they are protected by the same union as postal clerks.

You also want to be on the lookout for federal moose. I had a moose encounter once, when my wife and I were camping in Yellowstone National Park, which is popular with nature lovers because it has dangerous geysers of superheated steam that come shooting up out of the ground, exactly like in New York City, except that the Yellowstone geysers operate on a schedule. Anyway, one morning I woke up and went outside to savor the dawn's ever-changing subtle beauty, by which I mean take a leak, and there, maybe fifteen feet away, was an animal approximately the size of the Western Hemisphere and shaped like a horse with a severe steroid problem. It pretended to be peacefully eating moss, but this was clearly a clever ruse designed to lull me into believing that it was a gentle, moss-eating creature. Obviously no creature gets to be that large by eating moss. A creature gets to be that large by stomping other creatures to death with its giant hooves. Clearly what it wanted me to do was approach it, so it could convert me into a wilderness pizza while bellowing triumphant moss-breath bellows into the morning air. Fortunately I am an experienced woodsperson, so I had the presence of mind to follow the Recommended Wilderness Moose-Encounter Procedure, which was to get in the car and indicate to my wife, via a system of coded horn-honks, that she was to pack up all our equipment and put it in the car trunk, and then get in the trunk herself, so that I would not have to open the actual door until we had relocated to a safer area, such as Ohio.

This chilling story is yet another reminder of the importance of:

Selecting the Proper Campsite

Selecting the proper campsite can mean the difference between survival and death in the wilderness, so you, the woodsperson, must always scrutinize the terrain carefully to make sure that it can provide you with the basic necessities, the main one being a metal thing that sticks out of the ground where you hook up the air conditioner on your recreational vehicle. I'm assuming here that you have a recreational vehicle, which has been the preferred mode of camping in America ever since the early pioneers traveled westward in primitive, oxen-drawn Winnebagos.

Of course there are some thoughtful, environmentally sensitive ecology nuts who prefer to camp in tents, which are fine except for four things:

1. All tent-erection instructions are written by the Internal Revenue Service ("Insert ferrule post into whippet grommet, or 23 percent of your gross deductible adjustables, whichever is more difficult").

2. It always rains on tents. Rainstorms will travel thousands of miles against the prevailing winds for the opportunity to rain on a tent, which is bad because:

3. Tents contain mildews, which are tiny one-celled animals that are activated by moisture and immediately start committing one-celled acts of flatulence, so that before long it smells like you're sleeping in a giant unwashed gym sock.

4. Tents are highly attractive to bears. When bears are young, their parents give them, as a treat, little

camper-shaped candies in little tent wrappers.

So I'm recommending a major recreational vehicle, the kind that has a VCR-equipped recreation room and consumes the annual energy output of Syria merely to operate the windshield wipers. Other wilderness survival equipment that you should always take along includes:

▲ A hatchet, in case you need to fix the VCR

▲ Cheez-Its

▲ A flashlight last used in 1973, with what appears to be penicillin mold growing on the batteries

And speaking of penicillin, you need to know:

What to do in a medical Emergency

Experts agree that the most important rule in a wilderness medical emergency is: *Keep your head down on the follow-through.* No! My mistake! That's the most important rule in *golf.* The most important rule in a wilderness medical emergency is: *Don't panic.* To prevent the victim from going into shock, you must reassure him, as calmly as possible, that everything's going to be fine:

VICTIM *(clearly frightened):* Am I going to be okay?

YOU *(in a soothing voice):* Of course you are! I'm sure we'll find your legs around here someplace!

VICTIM *(relieved):* Whew! You got any Cheez-Its?

Once the victim has been calmed, you need to obtain pertinent information by asking the following Standard Medical Questions:

1. Does he have medical insurance?
2. Does his spouse have medical insurance?
3. Was he referred to this wilderness by another doctor?
4. How much does he weigh?
5. Does that figure include legs?

Write this information down on a medical chart, then give the victim a 1986 copy of Fortune magazine to read while you decide on the correct course of treatment. This will depend on the exact nature of the injury. For example, if it's mushroom poisoning or a broken limb, you'll need to apply a tourniquet. Whereas if it's a snake bite, then you need to determine whether the snake was poisonous, which will be indicated by tiny markings on the snake's stomach as follows:

WARNING! POISON SNAKE!
ACHTUNG! SCHLANGE SCHNAPPENKILLEN!

In this case. you need to apply a tourniquet to the snake, as shown in Figure 1.

Figure 1. Putting a tourniquet on a snake.

Fun Family Wilderness Activities

There are so many fun things for a family to do together in the wilderness that I hardly know where to start. One proven barrel of wilderness laughs is to try to identify specific kinds of trees by looking at the bark, leaves, federal identification plaques, etc. This activity is bound to provide many seconds of enjoyment for the youngsters. ("This one's an oak!" "No it's not!" "You suck!") Later on, you can play Survival Adventure, where the children, using only a compass and a map, must try to figure out what city Mom and Dad have driven to.

But the greatest camping fun comes at night, when everybody gathers 'round the campfire and sings campfire songs. Some of our "old family favorites" include:

I've Been Workin' on the Railroad
Oh, I've been workin' on the railroad,
With a banjo on my knee.
We will kill the old red rooster
We will kill the old red rooster
We will kill the old red rooster
And you better not get in our way.

Michael Row the Boat Ashore

Michael row the boat ashore, Alleluia!
Michael row the boat ashore, Alleluia!
Michael row the damn boat ashore, Alleluia!
Lenore threw up in the tackle box.

Camptown Races

Camptown ladies sing this song: Doo-dah,
  doo-dah
Camptown ladies been off their medication
And they are none too fond of the old red
  rooster, either.

After the singing, it's time for Dad to prepare
the children for bedtime by telling them a traditional campfire story. To qualify as traditional, the
story has to adhere to the following guidelines, es-
tablished by the National Park Service:

1. It has to begin Many Years Ago when some
   people camped Right in This Very Forest on a
   night Exactly Like Tonight.

2. People warned them not to camp here, but they
   paid no attention.

3. People said, "I wouldn't go back in there if I were you! That's the lair of the [select one]:
   a. Snake Man!"
   b. Swamp Devil!"
   c. Giant Radioactive Meat-Eating Box Turtle of Death!"

4. But the campers just laughed.

5. "Ha ha!" were their exact words.

6. Until they found little Jennifer's gallbladder on the Hibachi.

And so on. Dad should tell this story in a soft, almost hypnotic voice, lulling the children into a trance-like state in which they are aware of nothing except the story and the terror and the still, sinister darkness all around them and

OHMIGOD HERE
IT COMES

And then it's time for everybody to "call it a night" and climb, all five of you, into the sleeping bag with Mom.

Robert Benchley

"Knowing the Flowers" in
Chips Off the Old Benchley

A little learning may be a dangerous thing, but a lot of learning may turn out to be even worse. I have tried to know absolutely nothing about a great many things, and, if I do say so myself, have succeeded fairly well. And to my avoidance of the responsibilities which go with knowledge I lay my good digestion today. I am never upset when I find that I know nothing about some given subject, because I am never surprised.

The names of birds and flowers, for example, give me practically no worry whatever, for I never set out to learn them in the first place. I am familiar with several kinds of birds and flowers by sight, and could, if cornered, designate a carnation or a robin as such. But beyond that I just let the whole thing slide and never torture myself with trying to remember what the name of that bird with the yellow ear is or how many varieties of gentians there are. (By the way, what ever became of gentians? Are they used only for models in elementary school drawing classes?)

People who specialize in knowing the names of birds and flowers are always in a ferment, because they are always running up against some variety which stumps them. Show an ornithologist a bird that he can't name and he is miserable for a week. He goes home and looks up reference books, writes letters to the papers asking if someone can help him, and tosses and turns at night, hoping that his subconscious will solve the problem for him. He develops an inferiority and, unless closely watched, may actually do away with himself out of sheer frustration. It isn't worth it.

I once had a heart-breaking experience with a flower-namer. He was one of those men who began when they were boys spotting the different types of wild-flower, and, at a hundred yards, could detect a purple wolf's cup (or "Lehman's dropsy") and could tell you, simply by feeling a flower in the dark, which variety of "bishop's ulster" it was. There was practically no wild-flower of North America that he didn't know to speak to, and he took a little more pride in his knowledge than was really justified. At least, so it seemed to me.

I found myself on a walking trip through Cornwall with this man one summer, for, when he wasn't spying on wild-flowers, he was very good company. On account of the weather, we spent the first five days of our walking trip in the tap-room of an inn at a place appropriately named Fowey (pronounced Pfui), and on the first sunny day set out with our knapsacks on our backs and a good song ringing clear. Looking back on it now, I don't see what ever got into me to be doing so much walking.

Along about noon we came to a large field which was completely covered with multi-colored wild-flowers. There must have been a thousand different varieties, or, at any rate, a hundred. I saw what was coming and winced. I was going to be a party to a botany exam. Little did I realize that I was also to be a party to a tragedy.

My companion went over to the edge of the field

and examined a red flower by the roadside. His face took on a worried look. He didn't recognize the species! He looked at a blue flower next to it. He didn't recognize that, either! He gave a hurried survey of the five square feet surrounding him and blanched. He said nothing, but I could tell from his staring eyes and damp brow that there was not one variety of flower that he could name.

He ran into the field, stooping over and straightening up like a mad man, turning round and round in circles and looking wildly about him, as a dog looks when 10 people start whistling at him at once. Here was not only one flower that he had never heard of before, but a whole field full—hundreds and hundreds of unknown blossoms, all different and all staring up at him waiting to be named.

A chameleon is supposed to go insane when placed on a plaid. This man was in danger of going raving crazy from pure chagrin.

I tried to get him to leave the field and continue our little march, but he hardly heard what I was saying. He would pick a flower, examine it, shake his head, mop his brow, pick another, wipe the perspiration from his eyes, and then throw them both to the ground. Once he found something that he thought was a poppy and his joy was pitiful to see. But the stamen or something was wrong, and he burst into tears.

There was nothing that I could do or say, so I just sat by the roadside with my back turned and let him fight it out with himself. He finally agreed to leave his Waterloo, but the trip was ruined for him. He didn't speak all that day, and that night, after we had gone to bed, I heard him throwing himself about the bed in an agony of despair. He has never mentioned wild-flowers since.

I cite this little instance to show that being an expert in any one line is a tremendous responsibility. For, if an expert suddenly finds out that he isn't entirely expert, he just isn't anything at all. And that sort of thing gets a man down.

Tim Cahill

"Bad Advice" in
Jaguars Ripped My Flesh

Recently, I came across a survival manual issued to American troops in the South Pacific during World War II. The book contained a section on sharks that shimmered with falsehoods and sparkled with bad advice. At the time, soldiers and sailors had been hearing horror stories of shark attacks in the aftermath of several South Pacific maritime disasters. For instance, when the troop carrier *Cape San Juan* was torpedoed by a Japanese submarine, the merchant ship *Meredith* managed to rescue only a third of the fifteen hundred men who went down. The majority of those who died, according to eyewitness reports, were torn to shreds by sharks in a feeding frenzy. One rescuer, quoted in Michael Jenkinson's book, *Beasts Beyond the Fire*, said, "I heard soldiers scream as the sharks swept them off the rafts. Sometimes the sharks attacked survivors who were being hauled to the *Meredith* with life ropes.

In what Jenkinson thinks was an effort to "dispel shark fears among American troops," the survival manual stated flatly that sharks are "frightened by splashing" and easy to kill: Just stab the "slow-moving, cowardly" attacking shark in the belly. And, hey, why waste the chance to have a little fun in the bargain . . . . Swim out of line of his charge, grab a pectoral fin as he goes by, and ride with him as long as you can hold your breath."

This is real bad advice, and I was mulling it over early in October while camping and kayaking on the southeastern coast of Alaska. Specifically, I was thinking about the comforts of bad advice, and wondering what well-informed people do when confronted by an Alaskan brown bear.

These fellows weigh as much as fifteen hundred pounds and can stand nine feet tall. Your basic inland grizzly, by contrast, reaches a maximum height of seven feet and weighs about nine hundred pounds. For a time, the Alaskan brown was thought to be a separate species, but biologists are now satisfied that browns and grizzlies are different races within the same species, Ursus arctos. In other words, bad-news bears, because Ursus arctos of any race are aggressively unpredictable. Their fight-or-flight response leans heavily toward fight: The beasts evolved on the high plains and tundras, in competition with wolves, saber-tooths, and the like; with nowhere to hide, their best defense was a good offense. The American black bear, by contrast, evolved in the mountains and forests, in plenty of cover. With the exception of a sow with cubs, a black bear is likely to flee a threatening situation. Merely startle a grizzly, however, and instinct may launch him into an attack. And sometimes it seems to take even less than that.

In Yellowstone National Park, not far from where I live, it was an unusually bad year for grizzly attacks. On July 30, a grizzly dragged a young woman from her tent and killed her. In August, a Yellowstone grizzly mauled a twelve-year-old boy, and another injured a park naturalist and her husband. On September 4, two California campers survived a mauling in Glacier Park.

No one knows what caused the attacks, but some biologists studying Yellowstone grizzlies speculate about a lack of food: This was a lean year for high-country berries and white bark pine cones, they say, and the grizzlies may have been driven down into campsites in search of food. Others think that Yellowstone bears have become too accustomed to hikers and have lost their fear of man because fire-arms are not allowed in the park. Still others think that bears previously tranquilized with PCP—a drug that can cause violence in humans—have suddenly gone berserk on the drug. My own theory, which I began to develop as I thought about going up to Alaska, involves revenge. The Yellowstone bear population is declining disastrously. Soon it will be too small to support a self-sustaining population. I suspect that the few remaining beasts there can feel the black suction of extinction and are showing an existential rage beyond the capacity of their species. Perhaps they would he more benign where they were less threatened. Native Alaskans I talked to before my kayaking trip pointed out that there had been no maulings and no deaths all year in the area where I was going.

Still, my kayaking partner, photographer Paul
Dix, and I found it hard to be casual about the big
browns. We had agreed before the trip that we
wouldn't carry any fatty or odorous foods. Bears
don't see particularly well, and their hearing isn't
very keen, but they can apparently smell bacon several miles away. We cooked on the wave-washed
intertidal zone—in accord with Park Service regu-
lations—and stored our food a quarter-mile from
the tent, along with the clothes we wore for cooking. We had been told not to camp on an obvious
game trail, which seemed like a pretty self-evident
piece of information until a friendly ranger advised
us that our campsite—the beach just above the
high-tide line—was in fact the prime game trail.
So we camped in the tangled bush beyond the sand.
In the mornings, when we hiked inland to find our
food, we never failed to see tracks, mostly moose
and wolves. Then one day: the track of a bear so
huge it seemed prehistoric.

The alder breaks above the sand were jungle-
thick and just high enough to obscure our vision.
With an offshore wind blowing our scent out into
the ocean, we could easily stumble onto some

crabby, nearsighted, half-dead brownie. We tried to make plenty of noise, tried to give some bear ample warning that we were coming. We shouted as we walked. I adopted the dominant voice of unquestioned authority.

"Clear out, you pathetic wimps"

Paul, who is a gentle soul, added, "He doesn't really mean that, guys. We like bears."

After a few minutes of apologizing for me, Paul took to long explanations of why he wasn't actually with me.

All this seemed to be sensible enough, but what if we had the bad luck to stumble onto a bear anyway? Neither of us seemed to know what to do for certain. There were no trees within miles, and the head-high alder bushes would hardly support the weight of a man. Not much protection from a bear that stands nine feet tall on its hind legs. We needed a strategy.

Some people, I know, advocate playing dead. There is, for instance, a Montana rancher who was attacked by a grizzly two decades ago. The bear ripped most of this man's collarbone from his chest with one swipe. The rancher fell over and lay still, as if dead, all the while feeling the grizzly's hot breath on the back of his neck. "1 could smell her," he said. "She stunk like anything."

On the other hand, I had just read a new and authoritative book, *The Grizzly Bear*, by Thomas McNamee, who thinks that "playing dead may be a good idea once an attack is initiated. But I tend to think that playing dead before the bear exhibits any aggressive tendencies may in fact be an invitation." And then there was an old cartoon I remembered on the subject: Two bears were sitting around after dinner, picking their teeth and chatting. There was a backpack and hiking boot on the ground. One bear was saying, "Don't you just love it when they play dead?"

A privately published guidebook to the local trails carried the suggestion that we attempt to intimidate a bear by putting our arms around each other, in order to look like one big animal. Lumped together in this manner, we should speak to the bear in loud, dominant, and commanding voices. Somehow, this had the ring of riding sharks as long as you could hold your breath. Besides, Paul and I were philosophically divided as to what should be said.

Suppose I had Paul sit on my shoulders so we looked like some great tall animal. I'd be screaming, "You pathetic wimp!" while Paul would be trying to explain that, although he was sitting on my shoulders and all, we weren't really together.

And if that didn't work, it'd be pretty tough to run. I'd have to try psychology on the bear, all the while backing off slowly with Paul teetering on my shoulders. Maybe a little Freud would give the bear pause: "Uh, have you ever studied defense mechanisms? Like projection? Like, if I called you a pathetic wimp, see, it's not really you, it's me that's the pathetic wimp. . . ."

"I'm not with him!"

McNamee knows of cases where the one-big-animal approach has worked, but he has reservations about it. "I'd say Doug Peacock's method would be a better one. I can't think of anyone who's been closer to more grizzlies than Doug."

Peacock, who lived ten seasons with grizzlies in Yellowstone and Glacier parks, has been charged by more than a dozen different bears. "I stand my ground," he says. "I'm not saying this is foolproof or even recommending it. It's just always worked for me. So far."

Peacock bases his response on studies of inter-actions between the bears themselves. He's almost certain, for instance, that running will provoke an attack. Peacock tries to act like a self-confident bear who just doesn't feel like fighting today. "I stand sideways because I think confronting them full front is aggressive. I try not to look them in the eye for the same reason. 1 speak to them in a quiet voice. For some reason, I hold my arms out. I suppose it makes me look like a bigger animal, but I do it be-cause it feels right."

McNamee thinks Peacock's method is sound, but adds, "There could be something Doug hasn't figured into the equation. It could be as simple as the confidence he has in himself that someone else might lack. Then again, there could be something in that old Hemingway stuff about animals smell-ing fear."

When you're standing in the alder breaks after stepping over a monstrous bear track on the beach; when it's getting dark and there are suspicious . . . sounds . . . out in the bush; when there's no place to run or climb or hide; the fact that no one knows for sure how a human should act when confronted by a brown bear is not reassuring. Suddenly, I longed for something that would deliver supreme confidence. What we really needed here was some truly bad advice.

Frank B. Gilbreth, Jr. and Ernestine Gilbreth Carey

"Visiting Mrs. Murphy" *in Cheaper by the Dozen*

Roads weren't marked very well in those days, and Dad never believed in signs anyway.

"Probably some kid has changed those arrows around," he would say, possibly remembering his own youth. "Seems to me that if we turned that way, the way the arrow says, we'd be headed right back where we came from."

The same thing happened with the Automobile Blue Book, the tourist's bible in the early days of the automobile. Mother would read to him:

"Six-tenths of a mile past windmill, bear left at brick church and follow paved road."

"That must be the wrong windmill," Dad would say. "No telling when the fellow who wrote that book came over this road to check up on things.

28

My bump of direction tells me to turn right. They must have torn down the windmill the book's talking about."

Then, after he'd turned right and gotten lost, he'd blame Mother for giving him the wrong directions. Several times, he called Anne up to the front seat to read the Blue Book for him.

"Your Mother hasn't a very good sense of direction," he'd say loudly, glaring over his pince-nez at Mother. "She tells me to turn left when the book says to turn right. Then she blames me when we get lost. Now you read it to me just like it says. Don't change a single word, understand? And don't be making up anything about windmills that aren't there, or non-existent brick churches, just to confuse me. Read it just like it says."

But he wouldn't follow Anne's directions, either, and so he'd get lost just the same.

When things looked hopeless, Dad would ask directions at a store or filling station. He'd listen, and then usually drive off in exactly the opposite direction from the one his informant had indicated.

"Old fool," Dad would mutter. "He's lived five miles from Trenton all his life and he doesn't even know how to get there. He's trying to route me back to New York."

Mother was philosophical about it. Whenever she considered that Dad was hopelessly lost, she'd open a little portable ice box that she kept on the floor of the car under her feet, and hand Jane her bottle. This was Mother's signal that it was time to have lunch.

"All right, Lillie," Dad would say. "Guess we might as well stop and eat, while I get my bearings. You pick out a good place for a picnic."

While we were eating, Dad would keep looking around for something that might be interesting. He was a natural teacher and believed in utilizing every minute. Eating, he said, was "unavoidable delay." So were dressing, face-washing, and hair-combing. "Unavoidable delay" was not to be wasted.

If Dad found an ant hill, he'd tell us about certain colonies of ants that kept slaves and herds of cows. Then we'd take turns lying on our stomachs, watching the ants go back and forth picking up crumbs from sandwiches.

"See, they all work and they don't waste anything," Dad would say, and you could tell that the ant was one of his favorite creatures. "Look at the teamwork, as four of them try to move that piece of meat. That's motion study for you."

Or he'd point out a stone wall and say it was a perfect example of engineering. He'd explain about how the glaciers passed over the earth many years ago, and left the stone when they melted.

If a factory was nearby, he'd explain how you used a plumb line to get the chimney straight and why the windows had been placed a certain way to let in the maximum light. If the factory whistle blew, he'd take out his stopwatch and time the difference between when the steam appeared and when we heard the sound.

"Now take out your notebooks and pencils and I'll show you how to figure the speed of sound," he'd say.

He insisted that we make a habit of using our eyes and ears every single minute.

"Look there," he'd say. "What do you see? Yes, I know, it's a tree. But look at it. Study it. What do you see?"

But it was Mother who spun the stories that made the things we studied really unforgettable. If

Dad saw motion study and team-work in an ant hill, Mother saw a highly complex civilization governed, perhaps, by a fat old queen who had a thousand black slaves bring her breakfast in bed mornings. If Dad stopped to explain the construction of a bridge, she would find the workman in his blue jeans, eating his lunch high on the top of the span. It was she who made us feel the breathless height of the structure and the relative puniness of the humans who had built it. Or if Dad pointed out a tree that had been bent and gnarled, it was Mother who made us sense how the wind, beating against the tree in the endless passing of time, had made its own relentless mark.

We'd sit there memorizing every word, and Dad would look at Mother as if he was sure he had married the most wonderful person in the world.

Before we left our picnic site, Dad would insist that all of the sandwich wrappings and other trash be carefully gathered, stowed in the lunch box, and brought home for disposal.

"If there's anything I can't stand, it's a sloppy camper," he'd say. "We don't want to leave a single scrap of paper on this man's property. We're going to leave things just like we found them, only even more so. We don't want to overlook so much as an apple peel."

Apple peels were a particularly sore subject. Most of us liked our apples without skins, and Dad thought this was wasteful. When he ate an apple, he consumed skin, core and seeds, which he alleged were the most healthful and most delectable portions of the fruit. Instead of starting at the side and eating his way around the equator, Dad started at the North Pole, and ate down through the core to the South.

He didn't actually forbid us to peel our apples or waste the cores, but he kept referring to the matter so as to let us know that he had noticed what we were doing.

Sometimes, in order to make sure that we left no rubbish behind, he'd have us form a line, like a company front in the army, and march across the picnic ground. Each of us was expected to pick up any trash in the territory that he covered.

The result was that we often came home with the leavings of countless previous picnickers.

"I don't see how you children can possibly clutter up a place the way you do," Dad would grin as he stuffed old papers, bottles, and rusty tin cans into the picnic box.

"That's not our mess, Daddy. You know that just as well as we do. What would we be doing with empty whiskey bottles and a last year's copy of the Hartford *Courant*?"

"That's what I'd like to know," he'd say, while sniffing the bottles.

Neither Dad nor Mother thought filling station toilets were sanitary. They never elaborated about just what diseases the toilets contained, but they made it plain that the ailments were both contagious and dire. In comparison, leprosy would be no worse than a bad cold. Dad always opened the door of a public rest room with his coattail, and the preparations and precautions that ensued were "unavoidable delay" in its worst aspect.

Once he and Mother had discarded filling stations as a possibility, the only alternative was the woods. Perhaps it was the nervous strain of enduring Dad's driving; perhaps it was simply that fourteen persons have different personal habits. At any rate, we seemed to stop at every promising clump of trees.

"I've seen dogs that paid less attention to trees," Dad used to groan.

For family delicacy, Dad coined two synonyms for going to the bathroom in the woods. One was "visiting Mrs. Murphy." The other was "examining the rear tire." They meant the same thing.

After a picnic, he'd say:

"How many have to visit Mrs. Murphy?"

Usually nobody would. But after we had been under way ten or fifteen minutes, someone would announce that he had to go. So Dad would stop the car, and Mother would take the girls into the woods on one side of the road, while Dad took the boys into the woods on the other.

"I know every piece of flora and fauna from Bangor, Maine, to Washington, D.C.," Dad exclaimed bitterly.

On the way home, when it was dark, Bill used to crawl up into a swivel seat right behind Dad. Every time Dad was intent on steering while rounding a curve, Bill would reach forward and clutch his arm. Bill was a perfect mimic, and he'd whisper in Mother's voice, "Not so fast, Frank. Not so fast." Dad would think it was Mother grabbing his arm and whispering to him, and he'd make believe he didn't hear her.

Sometimes Bill would go into the act when the car was creeping along at a dignified thirty, and Dad finally would turn to Mother disgustedly and say:

"For the love of Mike, Lillie! I was only doing twenty."

He automatically subtracted ten miles an hour from the speed whenever he discussed the matter with Mother.

"I didn't say anything, Frank," Mother would tell him.

Dad would turn around, then, and see all of us giggling into our handkerchiefs. He'd give Bill a playful cuff and rumple his hair. Secretly, Dad was proud of Bill's imitations. He used to say that when Bill imitated a bird he (Dad) didn't dare to look up.

"You'll be the death of me yet, boy," Dad would say to Bill.

As we'd roll along, we'd sing three-and-four part harmony, with Mother and Dad joining in as soprano and bass. "Bobolink Swinging on the Bow," "Love's Old Sweet Song," "Our Highland Goat,"

"I've Been Working on the Railroad."

"What do only children do with themselves?" we'd think.

Dad would lean back against the seat and cock his hat on the side of his head. Mother would snuggle up against him as if she were cold. The babies were asleep now. Sometimes Mother turned around between songs and said to us: "Right now is the happiest time in the world." And perhaps it was.

Garrison Keillor

From "Winter" in *Lake Wobegon Days*

January, olden days. Jim and I were in the woods by the lake, talking about bears, and I was so scared, I had to pee. I unzipped my pants and took it out—he said, "Don't! It'll freeze! In midair!" just as I made the golden arc, and for one split second, I imagined it freezing and got so scared, I almost crapped. Even now, I sit up straight at the memory.

"Watch out for icicles," my mother said, but she didn't mean that icicle, she meant the fifty- and hundred-pounders that hung from the eaves, that came to a wicked sharp point. "One of those falls down, it could go right through your head." A huge one hung over the back door, and I thought about it when I put my boots on and stood with my hand on the knob. A boy on his way to school! A good boy! Being careful to slam the door shut behind

him, he loosens the giant icicle and its point, sharp
as an ice pick, slams all the way through his skull
and down into his heart, the huge butt of the mis-
sile splitting his head like a tomato. "He didn't stand
a chance," the sheriff said, standing over the small,
still form, one white hand still clutching a bookbag
that contained the dead boy's assignments, which
were posthumously awarded gold stars.

I left the house fast, escaping that death, but
other deaths waited for me. Icicles in the trees: you
couldn't watch out for them and watch out for holes
and bear traps. Holes in the ice on the river: you
couldn't see them under the snow, but one misstep
and suddenly you'd be in freezing water under the
ice, no way to come up for air. Holes in the ice on
the lake: we fished in them with a dropline, but what
if a giant snapper yanked on the line and pulled
you through? It was a small hole, and all your flesh
would come off.

Older children told stories about pump handles
and kids who put their tongues on them. You
put your tongue on a pump handle when it's so
bitterly cold, the spit freezes, you're stuck there.
Then either they pull you away, ripping your tongue

off, or else pitch a tent over you and wait for spring and hope for the best. It scared us little kids, the thought that one day during recess we might forget and put our tongue on the handle—who knows how these things happen? Maybe an older kid would make us do it. Maybe we would just forget—one moment of carelessness, and glurrp, you're stuck, and the teacher has to grab your head and, rrrrrrip, there's your little red tongue hanging from the handle. When you're little you believe that evil can somehow reach out and suck you in, so maybe you'd be lured toward that pump—maybe it would speak, "Hey kid, c'mere. Stick out your tongue," and put you in a trance.

So we little kids stayed away from behind the school where the pump was, and when we went out for recess, we kept our mouths shut. We did this, knowing also that a person who breathes through his mouth can freeze his lungs. You should always breathe through your nose: the nose warms up the air. You swallow air so cold through your mouth, suddenly there is a little chunk of ice in your chest where your lungs were. There are no last words when a person dies that way. You stand frozen in your tracks, a little blood leaks out your mouth, and you topple over in the snow.

One January morning, Rollie Hochstetter went in to town for a new belt for his woodsaw and got back home to find a couple dozen chickens, ducks, and geese strewn on the snow between the henhouse and the tool shed, their throats ripped open and blood spattered around where they'd been dragged and shaken, and all the other livestock in an uproar, even the Holsteins who looked like they'd been to the horror show. A pack of wild dogs did it. Rollie found dog tracks, and his neighbors said they had seen big dogs roaming in the woods, former pets who went bad, who hit Rollie's because he had no dog to guard the place since Rex died.

It was a caution to all, especially to us children who walk to Sunnyvale School just west of Rollie's, some of us with a half-mile hike each way. A lot crosses your mind when you're eight years old and the light is dim and the road goes through dark woods and there are wild dogs around, even if older children are with you.

In fact, it's worse with older children. They're the ones who say, as you trudge down the hill toward the ravine, "It's breakfast time for those dogs, you know. They're probably real hungry now. You know, they can smell food miles away. And they can tear your flesh off in about two minutes."

"They are more afraid of us than we are of them," you say, but you know it's not possible for a creature to be more afraid than this. "Not when they're hungry, they aren't," they say. "When they're hungry, they can run as fast as forty-three miles per hour, and they go straight for the throat, like this—" and someone screams in your ear and grabs your neck. *Cut it out! Leave me alone!*

You look down the road to the dark ravine, watching for slight branch movement, as if spotting the dogs would make a difference. You are dressed in a heavy snowsuit and boots like two club feet. You couldn't outrun a snow snake. Then they say, "If they do come, I think we should give them one of the little kids and maybe they'll let the rest of us go." And then one of them yells, "Here they come!" and they push you down in the ditch and everyone gallops down the road and through the ravine, girls screaming, lunchboxes banging.

Oh, yes, I remember that very well. I remember

who did it, and I'm sure they remember too. I don't get letters from those older children saying, "Sure enjoy your show. Remember me? We went to school together." They know I remember.

Winter is absolute silence, the cold swallows up sound except for your feet crunching and your heart pounding. And sharp cracks in the distance, which could be ice or trees or could be the earth itself. A planet with hot molten rock at the middle, that is frozen solid at the top—something has to give. The earth cracks wide open and people disappear in it. Limbs fall off trees and pin you to the ground. You walk into deep holes full of snow. You step into a bear trap covered with snow. Snap! it breaks your leg. You step into a deep hole, and there's a bear in it, a bear who has eaten nothing but dirt for weeks. He chews your arms off first and then eats your head.

Of course, if the Communists came, there wouldn't be anything you could do. They would line us up in the playground and give us a choice: either say you don't believe in God or else put your tongue on the pump handle. What would you do then? You could say, "I don't believe in God," and cross your fingers, but then how would God feel? Maybe He would turn you into a pillar of salt, like Lot's wife. Or an icicle.

After sixth grade, I left Sunnyvale and rode the bus in to Lake Wobegon High in town, where Mr. Detman was principal, a man who looked as if wild dogs were after him and a giant icicle hung over his head. Worry ate at Mr. Detman. He yelled at us when we ran downstairs, believing we would fall and break our necks and die on the landing. He imagined pupils choking on food and wouldn't allow meat in the lunchroom unless it was ground up. He had his own winter fear—that a blizzard would sweep in and school buses be marooned on the roads and children perish, so, in October, he announced that each pupil who lived in the country would be assigned a Storm Home in town. If a blizzard struck during school, we'd go to our Storm Home.

Mine was the Kloeckls', an old couple who lived in a little green cottage by the lake. She kept a rock garden on the lake side, with terraces of alyssum, pansies, petunias, moss roses, rising to a statue of the Blessed Virgin seated, and around her feet a bed of marigolds. It was a magical garden, perfectly arranged; the ivy on the trellis seemed to move up in formation, platoons of asters and irises along the drive, and three cast-iron deer grazed in front: it looked like the home of the kindly old couple that the children lost in the forest suddenly come upon in a clearing and know they are lucky to be in a story with a happy ending. That was how I felt about the Kloeckls, after I got their name on a slip of paper and walked by their house and inspected it, though my family might have wondered about my assignment to a Catholic home, had they known. We were suspicious of Catholics, enough to wonder if perhaps the Pope had ordered them to take in little Protestant children during blizzards and make them say the Rosary for their suppers. But I imagined the Kloeckls had personally chosen me as their storm child because they liked me. "Him!" they had told Mr. Detman. "In the event of a blizzard, we want that boy! The skinny one with the thick glasses!"

No blizzard came during school hours that year, all the snowstorms were convenient evening or weekend ones, and I never got to stay with the

Kloeckls, but they were often in my thoughts and they grew large in my imagination. My Storm Home. Blizzards aren't the only storms and not the worst by any means. I could imagine worse things. If the worst should come, I could go to the Kloeckls and knock on their door. "Hello," I'd say. "I'm your storm child."

"Oh, I know," she'd say. "I was wondering when you'd come. Oh, it's good to see you. How would you like a hot chocolate and an oatmeal cookie?"

We'd sit at the table. "Looks like this storm is going to last awhile."

"Yes."

"Terrible storm. They say it's going to get worse before it stops. I just pray for anyone who's out in this."

"Yes."

"But we're so glad to have you. I can't tell you. Carl! Come down and see who's here!"

"Is it the storm child??"

"Yes! Himself, in the flesh!"

Patrick F. McManus

"Get Lost" in *The Grasshopper Trap*

Several years ago I wrote what many experts consider the most authoritative work ever published on the topic of getting lost. The idea for the article germinated out of my observation that whereas millions of words have been written on how to survive when lost, absolutely nothing I had ever read dealt with the basic problem—how to get lost in the first place. What's the point of knowing how to survive if you don't know how to get lost?

Getting lost was a subject I knew firsthand. During my formative years, or approximately to age forty-five, I had deliberately contrived to discover all the various ways of getting lost, not only in the easy places, such as forests, mountains, and swamps, but also in less obvious terrain—vacant lots, shopping malls, parking garages, passenger trains, and tall buildings.

I discovered early in life that I had a natural talent for getting lost, a talent that through practice and discipline I honed to a sharp edge. By my mid-twenties I could set out for the corner grocery two blocks away from my house and, with practically no effort at all, end up several hours later in a trackless wasteland without the vaguest notion of how I had gotten there or how to get back. It reached the point where my wife would not allow me to go down to the basement to clean the furnace without map, compass, matches, and a three-day supply of food and water. I eventually compiled all my research on the subject of getting lost into an article entitled "The Modified Stationary Panic," which stands to this day, in the opinion of many, as the consummate work on the subject.

Although many scholars are satisfied to rest on their laurels, I am not. Several years passed without my becoming seriously lost even once, and I realized that I might lose the knack altogether, if I did not get out and do some fresh research. Thus, when my friends Vern and Gisela Schulze invited me along on a November deer-hunting trip in the snowy mountains north of their Idaho home, I quickly accepted.

The hunting trip started off in typical fashion. Vern assumed command and laid out the plans for the hunt, which included the admonition to me not to stray out of his sight. Vern and I have hunted, fished, and backpacked together ever since childhood, and I like to think that I have enriched his outdoor life immeasurably in providing him with countless hours of searching for me. Vern loves a good search.

Several opportunities to get lost offered themselves during the morning, but every time I thought to take advantage of them, either Vern or Gisela would come bounding out of the brush and herd me back to the trail. Then, about noon, I managed to give them the slip. I found a fresh set of deer tracks and followed them around the edge of a mountain—one of the best methods I've ever found for getting lost, and I highly recommend it. Soon the wind came up and snow began to fall, obliterating my own tracks so I couldn't retrace my trail, a nice bonus indeed! I can't begin to describe my elation upon suddenly stopping, peering around at the unfamiliar terrain, and discovering that I could still tell due north from my left elbow, but only because one of them itched

I immediately began to perform the Modified Stationary Panic, which consists of running madly in *place*, whooping and hollering as the mood dictates. The panic will thus conclude in the same spot it began, rather than, say, in the next state. The Modified Stationary Panic, one of my own inventions, eliminates chances for serious injury, as often occurs in the Flat-Out Ricochet Panic, and also does away with the need for your rescuers to comb a four-county area in their search for you.

No sooner had I completed the panic than Vern showed up. I did my best to conceal my disappointment.

"I thought you were lost," he said.

"No," I said. "I was right here."

"Good," he said. "Maybe you've finally outgrown the tendency. Anyway, I just spotted the fresh tracks of a big buck going up over the mountain, and I'm going to see if I can find him. You swing around the north edge of the mountain till you come to an old logging road. You can't miss it. When you hit the logging road, follow it back to the car and I'll meet you there."

"Right," I said.

Ha! Vern's mind was going bad. Here he had just presented me with the classic formula for getting lost, and he didn't even realize it. "The old logging road you can't miss" is one of the great myths of hunting lore.

As darkness closed in, accompanied by an icy, wind-driven rain, I found myself scaling a precipice in the presumed direction of the mythical logging road. My spirits had long since ceased to soar and were now roosting gloomily in my hungry interior. About halfway up the side of the cliff, I paused to study a loose rock in my hand and recognized it as one that was supposed to be holding me to the side of the mountain. My plummet into space was sufficiently long to allow me time for reflection, although on nothing of great philosophical significance. My primary thought, in fact, consisted of the rudimentary, "Boy, this is going to *hurt!*"

Sorting myself out from a tangle of fallen trees

at the bottom of the cliff, I took roll call of my various extremities, and found them present, with the
exception of the right leg. Rebellious by nature, the
leg now appeared to be absent without leave. Well,
I could not have been more gratified. Not only was
it getting dark and raining ice water, but I was in-
capacitated at the bottom of a canyon where no
one would ever expect me to be. Even so, sensing
that searchers might by luck find me too easily, I
struggled upright on my remaining leg, broke off a
dead tree limb for a crutch, and hobbled for another mile or so away from the beaten track. "Just
let them find me now," I muttered to myself, strug-
gling to restrain a smirk. "This is lost. This is real
honest-to-goodness lost. It may be years before
anyone finds me."

Detecting the onset of hypothermia, I built a
fire to keep warm. But that is to put it too simply,
too casually. No fire ever enjoyed such devoted attention. Cornea transplants are slapdash by comparison. The proceedings opened with a short religious service. Then pieces of tinder were recruited
individually, trained, and assigned particular duties. Over the tinder I placed larger pieces, some

approaching the size of toothpicks. At last the deli-
cate structure was ready for the match. And another
match. And still another match! I melted the snow
from the area with a few appropriate remarks, and
tried again to light the fire. This time it took. A
feeble, wispy little blaze ate a piece of tinder, gagged,
and nearly died. I gave it mouth-to-mouth resus-
citation. It struggled back to life, sampled one of
the toothpicks, found the morsel to its liking, and
ate another. The flame leaped into the kindling.
Soon the robust blaze devoured even the wet
branches I fed to it, first by the handful and then
by the armful. A mere bonfire would not do, I
wanted an inferno. A person lost in winter knows
no excess when it comes to his fire.

Next to the inferno, I built a lean-to with dead
branches pried from the frozen ground. I roofed
the lean-to with cedar boughs, and spread more
boughs on the ground for a bed. Well satisfied with
my woodcraft and survival technique, I stepped
back to admire the camp. "Heck, I could survive
here until spring," I said to myself. "Then again,
maybe only three hours."

Once the lost person has his inferno going and

his lean-to built, the next order of business is to think up witty remarks and dry comments with which to greet his rescuers. It's unprofessional to greet rescuers with stunned silence or, worse yet, to blurt out something like, "Good gosh almighty, I thought you'd never find me!" One must be cool, casual. Lying on the bed of boughs, next to the inferno, roasting one side of me and freezing the other, I tried to come up with some appropriate witticisms. "Dr. Livingstone, I presume," was one I thought rather good. Wishing to call attention to my successful fire-building technique, I thought I might try, "Did you bring the buns and wieners?" It is amazing how many witticisms you can think up while lying lost in the mountains. Two are about the limit.

I drifted off into fitful sleep, awakening from time to time to throw another log on the fire and check the darkness for Sasquatches. Suddenly, sometime after midnight, a voice thundering from the heavens jolted me awake. "Kneel! Kneel!" the voice roared.

So it has come to this, I thought. I stumbled to my feet and, wearing my lean-to about my shoulders, peered up into the darkness. A light was bouncing down the side of the canyon! And the voice called from above, "Neil! Neil! Have you found him?"

Within moments, Vern, Gisela, Neil, and the other members of the Boundary County Search and Rescue Team were gathered around me. It was a moving and dramatic scene, if I do say so myself. Calmly shucking off my lean-to, I tried to recall one of the witticisms I had thought up for the occasion. But the only one that came to mind was, "Good gosh almighty, I thought you'd never find me!" All things considered, that wasn't too bad.

Kathleen Meyer

From "Anatomy of a Crap" in
How to Shit in the Woods

High on a dusty escarpment jutting skyward from camp, a man named Henry, having scrambled up there and squeezed in behind what appeared to be the ideal bush for camouflage, began lowering himself precariously into a deep knee bend. Far below, just out of their bedrolls, three fellow river runners violated the profound quiet of canyon's first light by poking about the commissary, cracking eggs, snapping twigs, and sloshing out the coffee pot. Through the branches, our pretzel man on the hill observed the breakfast preparations while proceeding with his own morning mission. To the earth it finally fell, round and firm, this sturdy turd. With a bit more encouragement from gravity, it rolled slowly out from between Henry's big boots, threaded its way through the spindly trunks of the "ideal" bush, and then truly taking on a mind of its own, leaped into the air like a downhill skier out at the gate.

You can see the dust trail of a fast-moving pickup mushrooming off a dirt road long after you've lost sight of the truck. Henry watched, wide-eyed and helpless, as a similar if smaller cloud billowed up defiantly below him, and the actual item became obscured from view. Zigging and zagging, it caromed off rough spots in the terrain. Madly it bumped and tumbled and dropped, as though making its run through a giant pinball machine. Gaining momentum, gathering its own little avalanche, round and down it spun like a buried back tire spraying up sand. All too fast it raced down the steep slope—until it became locked into that deadly slow motion common to the fleeting seconds just preceding all imminent, unalterable disasters. With one last bounce, one final effort at heavenward orbit, this unruly goof ball (followed by an arcing tail of debris) landed in a terminal thud and a rain of pebbly clatter not six inches from the bare foot of the woman measuring out coffee.

With his dignity thus unraveled along sixty yards of descent, Henry in all likelihood might have come home from his first river trip firmly resolved to never again set foot past the end of the asphalt. Of course, left to his own devices and with any determination at all unless he was a total fumble-bum, Henry would have learned how to shit in the woods. Eventually. The refining of his skills by trial and error and the acquiring of grace, poise, and self-confidence—not to mention muscle development and balance—would probably have taken him about as long as it did me: years.

I don't think Henry would mind our taking a closer look at his calamity. Henry can teach us a lot, and not all by poor example. Indeed, he started out on the right track by getting far enough away from camp to ensure his privacy. Straight up just wasn't the best choice of direction. Next he chose a location with a view, although whether he took time to appreciate it is unknown. Usually I recommend a wide reaching view, a landscape rolling away to distant mountain peaks and broad expanses of wild sky. But a close-in setting near a lichen-covered rock, a single wildflower, or even dried up weeds and monotonous talus when quietly studied, can offer inspiration of a different brand.

The more time you spend in the wild, the easier it will be to reconnoiter an inspiring view. A friend of mine calls her morning exercise the Advanced Wilderness Appreciation Walk. As she strides along an irrigation canal practically devoid of vegetation, but overgrown with crumpled beer cans, has-been appliances, and rusted auto parts, she finds the morning's joy in the colors of the sunrise and the backlighting of a lone thistle.

Essential for the outdoor neophyte is a breathtaking view. These opportunities for glorious moments alone in the presence of grandeur should be soaked up. They are soul-replenishing and mind-expanding. The ideal occasion for communing with nature is while you're peacefully sitting still—yes, shitting in the woods. The rest of the day, unless you're trekking solo, can quickly become cluttered with social or organizational distractions.

But back to Henry, whose only major mistake was failing to dig a hole. It's something to think about: a small hole preventing the complete destruction of an ego. A proper hole is of great importance, not only in averting disasters such as Henry's, but in preventing the spread of disease and facilitating rapid decomposition. Chapter Two in its entirety is devoted to *the hole*.

More do's and don'ts for preserving mental and physical health while shitting in the woods will become apparent as we look in on Charles. He has his own notion about clothes and pooping in the wilderness: he takes them off. Needless to say, this man hikes well away from camp and any connecting trails to a place where he feels secure about completely removing his britches and relaxing for a spell. Finding an ant-free log, he digs his hole on the opposite side from the view, sits down, scoots to the back of the log, and floats into the rhapsody that pine tops find in the clouds. Remember this one. This is by far the dreamiest, most relaxing set up for shitting in the woods. A smooth, breadloaf-shaped rock (or even your backpack in a pinch in vacant wasteland) can be used in the same manner—for hanging your buns over the back.

This seems like an appropriate spot to share a helpful technique imparted to me one day by another friend: "Shit first, dig later." In puzzlement, I turned to her and as our eyes met she watched mine grow into harvest moons. But of course, "shit first, dig later"—that way you could never miss the hole. It was the perfect solution! Perfect, that is, for anyone with bad aim. Me? Not me.

Unlike Charles, there's my longtime friend Elizabeth who prizes the usefulness of her clothes. While on a rattletrap bus trip through northern Mexico, the lumbering vehicle on which she rode came to a five-minute halt to compensate for the lack of a toilet on board. Like a colorful parachute descending from the desert skies, Lizzie's voluminous skirts billowed to the earth, and she squatted down inside her own private outhouse.

Occasionally it is impossible to obtain an optimal degree of privacy. Some years back, my colleague Henrietta Alice was hitchhiking on the Autobahn in Germany, where the terrain was board flat and barren. At last, unable to contain herself, she asked the driver to stop and she struck out across a field toward a knoll topped by a lone bush. There, hidden by the branches and feeling safe from the eyes of traffic, she squatted and swung up the back of her skirt, securing it as a cape over her head.

But Henrietta's rejoicing ended abruptly. Out of nowhere came a column of Boy Guides (the rear guard?) marching past her bare derrière.

There are many theories on clothes and shitting, all individual and personal. In time you will develop your own. Edwin, our next case study, has a new theory about clothes after one memorable hunting trip; whether it be to take them off or keep them on, I haven't figured out.

For the better part of a nippy fall morning, Edwin had been slinking through whole mountain ranges of gnarly underbush in pursuit of an elusive six-pointer. Relentlessly trudging along with no luck, he finally became discouraged, a cold drizzle adding to his gloom. Then a lovely meadow opened before him and its beauty caused him to pause. His attention averted from the deer, he now relaxed into a gaze of pleasure, and soon became aware of his physical discomforts: every weary muscle, every labored joint, every minuscule bramble scratch— and then another pressing matter.

Coming upon a log beneath a spreading tree, Edwin propped up his rifle, quickly slipped off his poncho, and slid the suspenders from his shoulders. Whistling now, he sat and shat. But when he turned to bid it farewell, not a thing was there. Oh, hell! In total disbelief, Edwin peered over the log once more, still finding nothing. The sky opened and it began to rain and a pleasant vision of camp beckoned. Preparing to leave, he yanked on his poncho and hefted his gun. To warm his ears, he pulled up his hood. There it was! On the top of his head, melting in the rain like a scoop of ice cream left in the sun.

Poor Edwin will not soon forget this day; he walked seven miles before coming across enough water to get cleaned up. Though I fear he was in no humor to be thinking much beyond himself, we can only hope he did not wash directly in the stream. To keep pollutants from entering the waterways, it's important to use a bucket to haul wash water well above the high water line of spring runoff. But I digress . . .

Most of the foregoing stories are worst-case scenarios. I have recounted them not to scare you out of the woods, but to acknowledge the real perils and suggest how to work around them. Life itself is a risk; you could trip headlong over your own big toe or swallow your breakfast down the wrong pipe any day of the week. And have you *ever* tried to locate a toilet downtown—a task fraught with more frustration than any possible misfortune outdoors? Someone (not me) really needs to produce instructions for how to shit in the city.

I'll just say this: Disasters of elimination in the city can be more excruciatingly humiliating than those in the bush. Sometimes I think storekeepers, clerks, and tellers all must be terribly regular, "going" at home in the morning and then not needing a *terlit* (as my grandmother from Brooklyn would have said) for the rest of the day. If there is a stinking, grime-coated john tucked away in the far reaches of a musty storeroom, for some reason this information is as heavily guarded as the most clandestine revolutionary plans. In tramping around town, I've all too often encountered locked doors, scribbled *Out of Order* signs, *Emp1oyees Only* plaques, or "I'm sorry we don't have one" fibs. Sometimes, the only recourse is streak for home and hope to get there in time. I'll take the backcountry, thanks.

So, get on out there. Find a place of privacy, a

"place of easement" as the Elizabethans knew it. Find a panoramic view—one that can't be had with a Liberty quarter and the half turn of a stainless steel handle. Go for it!

A. A. Milne

"In Which Pooh and Piglet Go Hunting
and Nearly Catch a Woozle" in *Winnie-The-Pooh*

THE PIGLET lived in a very grand house in the middle of a beech-tree, and the beech-tree was in the middle of the forest, and the Piglet lived in the middle of the house. Next to his house was a piece of broken board which had: "TRESPASSERS W" on it. When Christopher Robin asked the Piglet what it meant, he said it was his grandfather's name, and had been in the family for a long time. Christopher Robin said you couldn't be called Trespassers W, and Piglet said yes, you could, because his grandfather was, and it was short for Trespassers Will, which was short of Trespassers William. And his grandfather had had two names in case he lost one—Trespassers after an uncle, and William after Trespassers.

"I've got two names," said Christopher Robin carelessly.

"Well, there you are, that proves it," said Piglet.

One fine winter's day when Piglet was brushing away the snow in front of his house, he happened to look up, and there was Winnie-the-Pooh. Pooh was walking round and round in a circle, thinking of something else, and when Piglet called to him, he just went on walking.

"Hallo!" said Piglet, "what are *you* doing?"

"Hunting," said Pooh.

"Hunting what?"

"Tracking something," said Winnie-the-Pooh very mysteriously.

"Tracking what?" said Piglet, coming closer.

"That's just what I ask myself. I ask myself, What?"

"What do you think you'll answer?"

"I shall have to wait until I catch up with it,"

said Winnie-the-Pooh. "Now, look there." He pointed to the ground in front of him. "What do you see there?"

"Tracks," said Piglet. "Paw-marks." He gave a little squeak of excitement. "Oh, Pooh! Do you think it's a—a—a Woozle?"

"It may be," said Pooh. "Sometimes it is, and sometimes it isn't. You never can tell with paw-marks."

With these few words he went on tracking, and Piglet, after watching him for a minute or two, ran after him. Winnie-the-

Pooh had come to a sudden stop, and was bending over the tracks in a puzzled sort of way.

"What's the matter?" asked Piglet.

"It's a very funny thing," said Bear, "but there seem to be two animals now. This-whatever-it-was—has been joined by another—whatever-it-is—and the two of them are now proceeding in company. Would you mind coming with me, Piglet, in case they turn out to be Hostile Animals?"

Piglet scratched his ear in a nice sort of way, and said that he had nothing to do until Friday, and would be delighted to come, in case it really *was* a Woozle.

"You mean, in case it really is two Woozles," said Winnie-the-Pooh, and Piglet said that anyhow he had nothing to do until Friday. So off they went together.

There was a small spinney of larch trees just here, and it seemed as if the two Woozles, if that is what they were, had been going round this spinney; so round this spinney went Pooh and Piglet after them; Piglet passing the time by telling Pooh what his Grandfather Trespassers W had done to Remove Stiffness after Tracking, and how his Grandfather

Trespassers W had suffered in his later years from Shortness of Breath, and other matters of interest, and Pooh wondering what a Grandfather was like, and if perhaps this was Two Grandfathers they were after now, and, if so, whether he would be allowed to take one home and keep it, and what Christopher Robin would say. And still the tracks went on in front of them....

Suddenly Winnie-the-Pooh stopped, and pointed excitedly in front of him. *"Look!"*

"What?" said Piglet, with a jump. And then, to show that he hadn't been frightened, he jumped up and down once or twice in an exercising sort of way.

"The tracks!" said Pooh. *"A third animal has joined the other two!"*

"Pooh!" cried Piglet. "Do you think it is another Woozle?"

"No," said Pooh, "because it makes different marks. It is either Two Woozles and one, as it might be, Wizzle, or Two, as it might be, Wizzles and one, if so it is, Woozle. Let us continue to follow them."

So they went on, feeling just a little anxious now, in case the three animals in front of them were of Hostile Intent. And Piglet wished very much that his Grandfather T. W. were there, instead of else-where, and Pooh thought how nice it would be if they met Christopher Robin suddenly but quite accidentally, and only because he liked Christopher Robin so much. And then, all of a sudden, Winnie-the-Pooh stoppeff again, and licked the tip of his nose in a cooling manner, for he was feeling more hot and anxious than ever in his life before. *There were four animals in front of them!*

"Do you see, Piglet? Look at their tracks! Three, as it were, Woozles, and one, as it was, Wizzle. *Another Woozle has joined them!*"

And so it seemed to be. There were the tracks; crossing over each other here, getting muddled up with each other there; but, quite plainly every now and then, the tracks of four sets of paws.

"I *think*," said Piglet, when he had licked the tip of his nose too, and found that it brought very little comfort, "I *think* that I have just remembered something. I have just remembered something that I forgot to do yesterday and shan't be able to do to-morrow. So I suppose I really ought to go back and do it now."

"We'll do it this afternoon, and I'll come with you," said Pooh.

"It isn't the sort of thing you can do in the after-noon," said Piglet quickly. "It's a very particular morning thing, that has to be done in the morn-ing, and, if possible, between the hours of —— What would you say the time was?"

"About twelve," said Winnie-the-Pooh, looking at the sun.

"Between, as I was saying, the hours of twelve

and twelve five. So, really, dear old Pooh, if you'll excuse me——*What's that?*"

Pooh looked up at the sky, and then, as he heard the whistle again, he looked up into the branches of a big oak-tree, and then he saw a friend of his.

"It's Christopher Robin," he said.

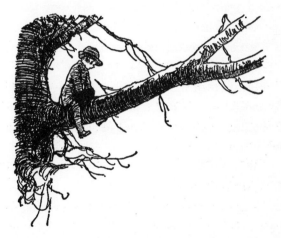

"Ah, then you'll be all right," said Piglet. "You'll be quite safe with *him*. Good-bye," and he trotted off home as quickly as he could, very glad to be Out of All Danger again.

Christopher Robin came slowly down his tree.

"Silly old Bear," he said, "what *were* you doing?

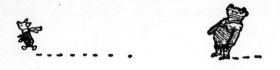

First you went round the spinney twice by yourself, and then Piglet ran after you and you went round again together, and then you were just going round a fourth time——"

"Wait a moment," said Winnie-the-Pooh, holding up his paw.

He sat down and thought, in the most thoughtful way he could think. Then he fitted his paw into one of the Tracks . . . and then he scratched his nose twice, and stood up.

"Yes," said Winnie-the-Pooh.

"I see now," said Winnie-the-Pooh.

"I have been Foolish and Deluded," said he, "and I am a Bear of No Brain at All."

"You're the Best Bear in All the World," said Christopher Robin soothingly.

"Am I?" said Pooh hopefully. And then he brightened up suddenly.

"Anyhow," he said, "it is nearly Luncheon Time."

So he went home for it.

Bill Oddie

From "Morocco" in *Follow That Bird!*

A true story. A bird-watcher was in love. He asked his sweetheart to marry him. She said 'yes', and eventually 'I will'. She was not a bird-watcher. They discussed where they should go for their honeymoon. She said she'd like to go somewhere warm but, being considerate–and realistic–she appreciated that it would be nice for him if wherever they went also had a few birds he could watch. He was grateful, whilst assuring her that bird-watching would most certainly be purely incidental on this trip. They settled on Cyprus in the spring. They arrived at their hotel, late in the afternoon of a beautiful balmy day in May. That evening, they enjoyed a romantic supper on the terrace. As they sipped their retsina and nibbled their kebabs, he barely noticed the flock of two hundred Bee-eaters circling above them, distracted as he was by the sparkle in his true love's eyes. The song of a nearby Great Reed Warbler was utterly drowned by her seductive whispers. Love is truly not only blind but also deaf, to all but the overwhelming promise of imminent passion. The setting sun bathed them in an irresistibly erotic glow as they rose from the table and moved towards the bridal suite. At the door, she paused. Not reluctant, but teasing, knowing that every second of delicious delay would merely heighten the bliss of eventual consummation. She nuzzled his ear: 'Join me in five minutes. I'm just going to slip into something more . . . .' She replaced the adjective with a smile that implied more than he'd ever dared imagine. He was left on the balcony to wait. Five minutes . . . to listen to his own heartbeat, to scan the stars, to smell the scented air, to smile at the moon, and to anticipate the moment when he and his lover would be reunited in the most meaningful–and, by the sound of it, extremely saucy–way. He looked at his watch. Half a minute to go. To pass the time he started counting the pebbles in the garden. One of them appeared to wink at him. A Nightjar perhaps. No . . . but it was surely a bird. Barely ten metres away. He couldn't resist it. He tiptoed towards it. It didn't move. He knelt and picked it up. He recognized the species immediately. It was dead, but in perfect condition. An immaculate specimen, worth keeping, if only as a memento of the most special of all nights. A night that was about to reach its climax.

'You can come in now,' she called.

He opened the door. The room was almost in darkness and yet the scene was gloriously and unashamedly visible. The lace curtains flapped gently at the window. Through them, the filtered moonlight directed an enticing spotlight inexorably towards . . . the bed. The quilt was turned back. The sheets were silk. And . . . there lay the lady. Her hair was spread out across the pillows, and she was spread out everywhere else. The diaphanous black négligé, which she had bought specially for this night, she had draped across her limbs so that it concealed just enough to be utterly, tantalizingly revealing. Her arms were loosely at her sides, but, as he gazed at her, she turned the palms of her hands upwards in the subtlest yet most irresistible of invitations. It was a moment she had planned for months, maybe years, maybe all her life.

'Well?' she whispered, and closed her eyes, awaiting his response. When she opened them again, he had disappeared. He was in the kitchen.

'I'll be with you in a minute, darling, I'm just skinning a Short-toed Lark.'

Well, OK, maybe I've added a few touches of the Barbara Cartlands—or was it Jackie Collinses?— and maybe it wasn't Cyprus, but it *was* a Short-toed Lark and, basically, it *did* happen. I presume the story was related by the wife to the lawyers, as grounds for an instant divorce. Or maybe it was the bird-watcher's defence.

'Oh come on. Surely you can appreciate my dilemma? A perfect specimen of a Short-toed Lark. I mean, I know it was *dead* and it wasn't going to fly away or anything but, if I'd left it, it could have gone off. It was a very warm night, and the fridge hadn't been switched on, so I couldn't put it in there. And, be honest, she did look as if she was set for quite a long session, and, anyway, I usually fall asleep afterwards and then I wouldn't have got round to skinning it till next morning. And, let's face it, even if I had just left it by the side of the bed and got on with the "business", I know I wouldn't have been able to concentrate. I'd've just wanted to get it over with so I could get back to the lark. Or I might not have been able to do anything at all actually, and she wouldn't have been very happy about that, would she? I mean, I did go back in as soon as I'd finished skinning it, but she said she found the lark's blood under my fingernails really off-putting. And I did try and make it up to her next morning by bringing her breakfast in bed, but unfortunately I'd forgotten I'd put the corpse in the yoghurt pot, 'cos it was the only thing I could find that was airtight. She didn't have to keep screaming like that, though. It isn't as if she took a bite out of it! Anyway, I reckon I could divorce *her* for withholding my conjugal rights. I tell you, that was the only lark I had on *that* honeymoon!'

Now I dare say that you are expecting me to confess at this moment that I was that bird-watcher, and that the lady was my ex-wife. But no. Believe me, if it had been me, I wouldn't be telling you about it. So why did I relate that story? Well, merely to illustrate that bird-watchers can be pretty obsessive, perhaps to the point of grotesque insensitivity, and certainly to the point of neglect of spouses and children. There are plenty of birding widows and orphans, but I hope that *my* wife or children would not complain that they are amongst them. I like to think that I've got things reasonably in proportion. By way of some kind of evidence in support of this claim, I offer the fact that we often manage to share family holidays–something which I know some birders and their families find almost impossible to do. The birders feel unbearably constrained if they are not constantly allowed out birding, and the families feel understandably neglected if they are constantly being left. The answer, of course, has to be a compromise, something which, alas, birders seem to find harder to achieve than families. That I think I *have* achieved it myself, I admit, owes a great deal to the fact that I have a very tolerant wife (Laura) and daughter (Rosie), who also have enough sense of self-preservation to know that I would be totally unbearable if I were not unleashed now and again.

For what it's worth, a quick guide to sharing happy holidays for birders and non-birding families would involve some of the following tips:

From the non-birding woman's point of view, probably the most efficient solution would be to marry a man so tedious that you have no wish to spend any time at all with him on holiday anyway. Then you'll be positively grateful if he keeps going off bird-watching. The problem is that you'll probably go off him pretty rapidly as well.

So seriously folks.... This advice is aimed at the birders. (Usually male, though I'm not really sure why.) Make sure you go somewhere nice, at a time when the weather is going to be warm enough to spend time on a beach or in a pool (or even the sea, if you want to risk it). Decisions on what is 'nice' in terms of place and time must involve a ruthless degree of honesty from the birder. A windswept promontory with a sewage farm and a power-station on it might well be great for birding, but not for sunbathing. Even Cyprus–or any other Mediterranean country–isn't guaranteed to be 'good for sunbathing' if you go too early in the spring. As a general rule: if it's 'just right' for a bird-watcher, it's too cold for the family. Conversely, if it's 'just right' for the family, it's probably too hot for birding. The way to please everyone is to go to a hot country but

rise early, when it's still cool and, as it happens, the
birds are most active. Go birding for a few hours,
but try to get back when the family are getting up.
Then spend the day *en famille* and–if you can bear
it–without binoculars. At the end of the day, nip
off for a brief evening excursion, but make sure
you're back in time to organize the evening meal,
which should be taken fairly late, and with plenty
of wine, so that everyone sleeps in the next morning. Except, of course, *you*, who have to be up at
dawn to go birding again. And so on. If possible,
also plead for one 'big day out' each week. You could
trade this off for a 'big day out' for the family, doing something you probably don't really want to
do, like looking at markets or ruins. Keep an open
mind, and you might even find you rather enjoy
these things. You might even come to realize that
there's more to life than birds!

Bill Richardson

"Brief Lives: Gordon" in
Bachelor Brothers' Bed and Breakfast

For a long time, I never saw the humour in the phrase "I found myself lost." As in, "Halfway down the road of life, I found myself lost in a dark wood." The irony only hit home when it happened to me.

I remember when. It was about a month after the morning I looked at myself in the bathroom mirror—I was shaving—and saw I had turned into my father. It gave me a start. But on reflection (no pun intended), I saw it was inevitable. I'd patterned my whole life on his. Even as a little boy, I knew I'd follow the trail he'd blazed. Study hard. Go to law school. Work like a sonofabitch. And that's what happened.

Through his old boy connections, I got articles with a big downtown firm. I became an associate, worked thirteen-hour days, seven days a week, was a partner by the time I was thirty. Somehow, I managed to meet and marry a woman who didn't mind that her husband was a stranger. She was content to raise our two children without any assistance or input from me. Other than that required by biology. It was a way of life. We chose it. In our own way, we were happy.

One partner in the firm was an attorney whose only passion, other than law, was the great outdoors. She loved nothing more than heading into the wilderness with a kayak, a compass, a Swiss army knife, and a bar of bitter chocolate. She was fierce and used to getting her own way. It was at her suggestion—or insistence—that the senior partners in the firm came to the rather extraordinary agreement that we would go off together one weekend for a wilderness adventure.

"The organization that directs these retreats is used to dealing with inexperienced outdoorsmen. They won't throw you into impossible situations. You'll be challenged without being in danger. And there are group activities that will help us learn to work together in new ways. It'll be a growth experience," she said, cracking her knuckles. An impressive array of sinewy cables ran the length of her forearms.

So we came to this island: seven lawyers with six-figure incomes. None of us had ever seen any of the others dressed in anything but business attire. We arrived at a lodge on Friday evening and were advised to retire early. The next day would be hard slogging.

On Saturday morning, we were wakened before dawn, fed a spartan breakfast, herded into a large 4 x 4 van, and driven along a rut-ridden logging trail. Halfway to nowhere, and halfway down the road of life, we disembarked and stood under the dwarfing trees, listening to the instructions of our wilderness leader, a lean young man called Solstice.

"Welcome to the forest! Tomorrow, you'll be spending the whole day alone here! Today, we'll be doing some preparatory exercises! First, we'll seek out the inner wilderness. Go into the bush, as far as you feel comfortable! Crawl along the ground. Feel the earth with your belly, like a snake! Taste the soil, like a worm! Hug the trees, like a bear! Howl, like a wolf! Ask Nature to tell you her secrets. Come back in twenty minutes, and we'll share our experiences."

None of us looked at the others. Only the partner whose brainchild this was demonstrated immediate enthusiasm. She flung herself on all fours, threw back her head, ululated to the rising sun, and scuttled into the undergrowth. The rest of us wandered, rather disconsolately, into the tangle of green.

I walked for about five minutes: directionless, overwhelmed by the sense of being an alien in this place. The natural world was utterly foreign to me. I couldn't name any of the plants or trees I saw around me, except to say: Conifer. Moss. Fern. The silence was unsettling. When had I last been alone with my thoughts? There was nothing to listen to but birdsong and the useless hum and rattle of my own brain. In the distance, I heard a strangely accented yapping. One of my colleagues, I supposed, getting into the spirit of the exercise.

I was in the woods. But I felt completely at sea. How, I wondered, had a group of hard-nosed professionals been so easily sold this New Age bill of goods? Why were we risking life and limb to please some neo-pagan park ranger wannabe? "Arf, arf," I muttered under my breath. I threw my arms around the wide girth of an indifferent-looking tree. Why not? There was nothing else to do.

"Okay, tree," I said. "Give! Tell me something I need to know." I snickered. But I didn't let go. It felt good, much to my surprise, to hug this tree, which was old and full of the stuff of support. It was unexpectedly settling, like being anchored and buoyed at the same time.

A few minutes passed, and still I held on. The tree was a pine, or a fir, or a cedar. For me, the distinctions are hazy. The bark was raspy, slightly sticky. Resin. I breathed in the smell of Christmas.

"Tell me," I said, again, "tell me something I need to know."

This time the tree spoke. Its voice came up from its roots, rising up through its tight and many rings. It said, "Get the hell out."

If you've heard a tree talk, you'll know that you don't argue or cross-examine. You do what you're told.

I was not in prime condition. It had been a long time since I had run. So, I was surprised it came so easily. Fleet footed and full of wind, I raced over the thick carpet of needles, jumping roots and dodging branches, pelting back towards the trail. I had forgotten that in my athletic high school days, when I had competed in track events, I would drive myself on by grunting out a syllabic rendition of the Lone Ranger segment of "The William Tell Overture." Memory lives in our muscles, though, as much as in our skulls. As I pushed forward, I found myself singing, for the first time in twenty years, "Nunga nung, Nunga nung, Nunga Nung Nung Nung!"

I was elated, strong, invulnerable. I leapt out of the woods, running on velvet paws, a rekindled fire in my belly and groin sparking me on. The van was empty. There was still no sign of my colleagues, who were out in the trees looking for what I had some-how found. Solstice was nowhere to be seen. I didn't pause to consider where I was going or why. It was unimportant. A tree had given me instructions, and I was following them.

I followed the ruts left by logging trucks, run-ning faster and faster on the downhill grade: foot and ankle, shin and knee, thigh and pelvis working on a single circuit, my arms pumping like the surprised Icarus, chest heaving. It was as if I had a whole herd of bison in me, stampeding with a collective death wish towards the edge of a cliff.

I reached the point where the logging trail intersected with the main road—morning mist rising up from black asphalt—considered for a second the option of left or right, and collapsed like a diseased lung.

And that was where Hector found me, curled up foetally on the grassy narrow, my face scratched by branches, my left ankle swelling. It had twisted beneath me when I fell.

"Thought the worst," he said, once I had come to. "You wouldn't win any beauty contests just at the minute. What happened?"

And I told him the whole story, sparing no detail. Had someone suggested to me, only a day before, that I would both hear a tree talk and confess the hallucination to a total stranger: well, I would have said he was mad. Nonetheless, there I was, clutching a thermos cup of black coffee in my shaking hands, blood drying on my face, a pulsing pain running up my leg, telling this Good Samaritan that I had been hearing voices in the forest.

"It said to me, 'Get the hell out.' I guess I hadn't thought about where I was getting the hell out to."

Hector let this settle in.

"Maybe," he said, "you misread the punch line."

"I'm sorry?"

"In my experience, which is slight, trees say just what they mean. No more. No less. It didn't say 'Get the hell out of my forest.' It told you to 'Get the hell out.' That's something else again. Get it?"

I was too exhausted, too sore, to take much of this in. I shook my head and took another gulp of coffee.

"No," I said, "I don't get it at all."

"Not to worry. It can take a long time. Speaking of time, your friends must be out of their minds with worry. Up that road?"

I don't have much recollection of what followed. I was too drained to feel anything like shame, or even interest, in what might happen next. My colleagues were, as Hector predicted, quite frantic by the time we rolled up to the van. No doubt they had enjoyed all kinds of bloody imaginings: Bears. Cougars.

I had become entirely passive. I sat in the cab of

Hector's pickup while he negotiated my immediate future. The other partners looked from me to
him and back again. We never spoke. I gave them a
halfhearted wave and a wan smile. I don't know
what he told them. In the end, though, I was
brought here, to the Bachelor Brothers' Bed and
Breakfast, and installed in a comfortable bed with
an ice pack on my ankle.

"My brother, Virgil," Hector said by way of in-
troduction. "Virgil, what book would you suggest
for someone who was told by a tree to get the hell
out?"

Virgil considered this for a long minute or two.

"Not Dante. But the Hardy Boys might be a good
bet. And give him a whisky, quick. Whisky's cura-
tive properties are diluted by half if it's given after
noon."

That was the first of my several visits with the
Bachelor Brothers, two years ago now. I stayed on
for four days, reading about the adventures of Frank
and Joe in secret passages and hidden caves, in
smugglers' coves and lost canyons. In my waking
hours and in my dreams, I shared their perfect lives,
their well-ordered and moral universe where noth-

ing changed and trees were never known to talk.

On the Monday afternoon, I decided I would change my name and move to Mexico. But the next day was Tuesday. Ever noticed how the world can seem different on Tuesday? I decided to go back to my family, back to the firm, and begin the hard and real work of getting the hell out. Hector drove me to the ferry. When I stepped from the truck, I caught a glimpse of myself in the side mirror. The cuts on my face were largely healed. I hardly recognized the man who looked back at me.

That's what happened to me. No one will believe any of it. Sometimes, life's like that.

Howard Tomb

From "Fine Points of Expedition Behavior" in
The Cool of the Wild

A good expedition team is like a powerful, well-oiled, finely tuned marriage. Members cook together, carry burdens together, face challenges together, and finally go to bed together.

A bad expedition, on the other hand, is an awkward, ugly, embarrassing thing characterized by bickering, filth, frustration, and crunchy macaroni.

Nearly all bad expeditions have one thing in common: poor expedition behavior (EB). This is true even if team members follow the stated rules.[1]

Unfortunately, too many rules of expedition behavior remain unspoken. Some leaders seem to assume that their team members have strong and

---

[1] Such as Don't Step on the Rope, Separate Kerosene and Food, No Soap in the River , No Raccoons in the Tent, Keep Your Ice Axe Out of My Eye, etc.

generous characters like their own. But many would-be woodspeople need more rules spelled out. Here are ten of them.

RULE NO. 1:
GET THE HELL OUT OF BED.

Suppose your tentmates get up early to fetch water and fire up the stove while you lie comatose in your sleeping bag. As they run an extensive equipment check, coil ropes, and fix your breakfast, they hear you begin to snore.

Last night you were their buddy; now they're drawing up a list of things about you that make them want to spit. They will devise cruel punishments for you. You deserve them.

RULE NO. 2: DO NOT BE
CHEERFUL BEFORE BREAKFAST.

Some people wake up as happy and perky as fluffy bunny rabbits. They put stress on those who wake up as mean as rabid wolverines.

Exhortations such as "Rise and shine, sugar!" and "Greet the dawn, pumpkin!" have been known to provoke pungent expletives from wolverine types. These curses, in turn, may offend bunny rabbit types. Indeed they are issued with the intent to offend. Thus the day begins with flying fur and hurt feelings.

The best early-morning EB is simple: be quiet.

RULE NO. 3: DO NOT COMPLAIN.
ABOUT ANYTHING. EVER.

Visibility is four inches, it's -10 F, and wind-driven hailstones are embedding themselves in your face like shotgun pellets. Must you mention it? Do you think your friends haven't noticed the weather? Make a suggestion. Tell a joke. Lead a prayer. Do not lodge a complaint.

Yes, your pack weighs eighty-seven pounds and your cheap backpack straps are actually cutting into your flesh. Were you promised a personal Sherpa? Did someone cheat you out of a mule team? If you can't carry your weight, get a motor home.

RULE NO. 4: LEARN TO
COOK AT LEAST ONE THING WELL.

One expedition trick is so old it is no longer amusing: on the first cooking assignment the clever "chef" prepares a dish that resembles, say, Sock du Sweat en Sauce de Waste Toxique. The cook hopes to be permanently relieved of cooking duties.

This is a childish approach to a problem that's been with us since people first started throwing lizards on the fire. Tricks are not in the team spirit. If you don't like to cook, offer to wash dishes and prepare the one thing you do know how to cook. Even if it's only tea.

Remember: talented camp cooks sometimes get invited to join major Himalayan expeditions, all expenses paid.

RULE NO. 5:
EITHER SHAMPOO OR DO NOT REMOVE YOUR HAT FOR ANY REASON.

After a week or so without shampoo and hot water, hair becomes a mass of angry clumps and wads. These leave the person beneath looking like an escapee from a mental institution. Such an appearance may shake your team's confidence in your judgment.

If you can't shampoo, pull a cap down over your ears and leave it there, night and day, for the entire expedition.

RULE NO. 6: DO NOT ASK
IF ANYBODY'S SEEN YOUR STUFF.

Experienced adventurers have systems for organizing their gear. They very rarely leave it strewn around camp or lying back on the trail. One of the most damning things you can do is ask your teammates if they've seen the tent poles you thought you packed twenty miles ago. Even in the event you get home alive, you will not be invited on the next trip.

Should you ever leave tent poles twenty miles away, do not ask if anybody's seen them. Simply announce—with a good-natured chuckle—that you are about to set off in the dark on a forty-mile hike to retrieve them.

RULE NO. 7: NEVER ASK "WHERE
ARE WE?" OR "HOW MUCH LONGER?"

If you want to know your location, look at a map. Try to figure it out yourself. If you're still confused, feel free to discuss the identities of landmarks around you and how they correspond to the cartography.

Now, if you (a) suspect a mistake has been made

and (b) have experience reading topographical maps *and* (c) are certain that your leader is a novice or on drugs, speak up. Otherwise, follow the group like a sheep.

RULE NO. 8: CARRY MORE
THAN YOUR FAIR SHARE.

When the trip is over, would you rather be remembered fondly as a rock or scornfully as a wussy? Keep in mind that a few extra pounds won't make your pack more painful than it already is.

In any given group of flatlanders, somebody is bound to bicker about weight. When an argument begins, take the extra weight yourself. Shake your head and gaze with pity on the slothful one. This is the mature response to childish behavior. On the trail that day, load the greenhorn's pack with twenty pounds of gravel.

RULE NO. 9: DO NOT GET SUNBURNED.

Sunburn is not only painful and unattractive; it's also an obvious sign of inexperience. Most bozos wait too long before applying sunscreen.

Once you're burned on an expedition, you may

not have a chance to get out of the sun. The burn will get burned, skin will peel away, blisters will sprout on the already swollen lips . . . you get the idea.

Wear zinc oxide. You can see exactly where and how thickly it's applied, and it gives you just about 100 percent protection. It does get on your sunglasses, all over your clothes, and in your mouth. But that's OK. Unlike sunshine, zinc oxide is non-toxic.

RULE NO. 10: DO NOT GET KILLED.

Suppose you make the summit of K2 solo, chain-smoking Gitanes and carrying the complete works of Hemingway in hardcover. Macho, huh?

Suppose that you then take a vertical detour into the jaws of a crevasse and never make it back to base camp. Would you still qualify as a hero? And what if you do? No one is going to run any fingers through your new chest hair.

The worst thing to have on your outdoor résumé is a list of the possible locations of your remains. Besides, your demise might distract your team members from enjoying the rest of their vacation.

All expedition behavior flows from one principle: think of your team first. You are merely a cog in that machine. If you're unable to be a good cog, your team will never have more than one member[2]—and you will never achieve suavity.

---

[2]A penile member

Mark Twain

From Chapter XXXII-XXXIII in *Roughing It*

Chapter XXXII

We seemed to be in a road, but that was no proof. We tested this by walking off in various directions— the regular snow-mounds and the regular avenues between them convinced each man that *he* had found the true road, and that the others had found only false ones. Plainly the situation was desperate. We were cold and stiff and the horses were tired. We decided to build a sage-brush fire and camp out till morning. This was wise, because if we were wandering from the right road and the snow-storm continued another day our case would be the next thing to hopeless if we kept on.

All agreed that a camp fire was what would come nearest to saving us, now, and so we set about building it. We could find no matches, and so we tried to make shift with the pistols. Not a man in the party had ever tried to do such a thing before, but not a man in the party doubted that it *could* be done, and without any trouble—because every man in the party had read about it in books many a time and had naturally come to believe it, with trusting simplicity, just as he had long ago accepted and believed *that other* common book-fraud about Indians and lost hunters making a fire by rubbing two dry sticks together.

We huddled together on our knees in the deep snow, and the horses put their noses together and bowed their patient heads over us; and while the feathery flakes eddied down and turned us into a group of white statuary, we proceeded with the momentous experiment. We broke twigs from a sage bush and piled them on a little cleared place in the shelter of our bodies. In the course of ten or fifteen minutes all was ready, and then, while conversation ceased and our pulses beat low with anxious suspense, Ollendorff applied his revolver, pulled the trigger and blew the pile clear out of the county! It was the flattest failure that ever was.

This was distressing, but it paled before a greater

horror—the horses were gone! I had been appointed to hold the bridles, but in my absorbing anxiety over the pistol experiment I had unconsciously dropped them and the released animals had walked off in the storm. It was useless to try to follow them, for their footfalls could make no sound, and one could pass within two yards of the creatures and never see them. We gave them up without an effort at recovering them, and cursed the lying books that said horses would stay by their masters for protection and companionship in a distressful time like ours.

We were miserable enough, before; we felt still more forlorn, now. Patiently, but with blighted hope, we broke more sticks and piled them, and once more the Prussian shot them into annihilation. Plainly, to light a fire with a pistol was an art requiring practice and experience, and the middle of a desert at midnight in a snow-storm was not a good place or time for the acquiring of the accomplishment. We gave it up and tried the other. Each man took a couple of sticks and fell to chafing them together. At the end of half an hour we were thoroughly chilled, and so were the sticks. We bitterly execrated the Indians, the hunters and the books that had betrayed us with the silly device, and wondered dismally what was next to be done. At this critical moment Mr. Ballou fished out four matches from the rubbish of an overlooked pocket. To have found four gold bars would have seemed poor and cheap good luck compared to this. One cannot think how good a match looks under such circumstances—or how lovable and precious, and sacredly beautiful to the eye. This time we gathered sticks with high hopes; and when Mr Ballou prepared to light the first match, there was an amount of interest centred upon him that pages of writing could not describe. The match burned hopefully a moment, and then went out. It could not have carried more regret with it if it had been a human life. The next match simply flashed and died. The wind puffed the third one out just as it was on the imminent verge of success. We gathered together closer than ever, and developed a solicitude that was rapt and painful, as Mr. Ballou scratched our last hope on his leg. It lit, burned blue and sickly, and then budded into a robust flame. Shading it with his hands, the old gentleman bent gradually down and every heart went with him—everybody, too, for that matter—and blood and breath stood still. The flame touched the sticks at last, took gradual hold upon them—hesitated—took a stronger hold—hesitated again—held its breath five heart-breaking seconds, then gave a sort of human gasp and went out.

Nobody said a word for several minutes. It was a solemn sort of silence; even the wind put on a stealthy, sinister quiet, and made no more noise than the falling flakes of snow. Finally a sad-voiced conversation began, and it was soon apparent that in each of our hearts lay the conviction that this was our last night with the living. I had so hoped that I was the only one who felt so. When the others calmly acknowledged their conviction, it sounded like the summons itself. Ollendorff said:

"Brothers, let us die together. And let us go without one hard feeling towards each other. Let us forget and forgive bygones. I know that you have felt hard towards me for turning over the canoe, and for knowing too much and leading you round and round in the snow—but I meant well; forgive me. I acknowledge freely that I have had hard feelings against Mr. Ballou for abusing me and calling me a logarythm, which is a thing I do not know what, but no doubt a thing considered disgraceful and unbecoming in America, and it has scarcely been out of my mind and has hurt me a great deal—but let it go; I forgive Mr. Ballou with all my heart, and—"

Poor Ollendorff broke down and the tears came. He was not alone, for I was crying too, and so was Mr. Ballou. Ollendorff got his voice again and forgave me for things I had done and said. Then he got out his bottle of whisky and said that whether he lived or died he would never touch another drop. He said he had given up all hope of life, and although ill-prepared, was ready to submit humbly to his fate; that he wished he could be spared a little longer, not for any selfish reason, but to make a thorough reform in his character, and by devoting himself to helping the poor, nursing the sick, and pleading with the people to guard themselves against the evils of intemperance, make his life a beneficent example to the young, and lay it down at last with the precious reflection that it had not been lived in vain. He ended by saying that his reform should begin at this moment, even here in the presence of death, since no longer time was to be vouchsafed wherein to prosecute it to men's help and benefit—and with that he threw away the bottle of whisky.

Mr. Ballou made remarks of similar purport, and began the reform he could not live to continue, by throwing away the ancient pack of cards that had solaced our captivity during the flood and made it bearable. He said he never gambled but still was satisfied that the meddling with cards in any way was immoral and injurious, and no man could be wholly pure and blemishless without eschewing them. "And therefore," continued he, "in doing this act I already feel more in sympathy with that spiritual saturnalia necessary to entire and obsolete reform." These rolling syllables touched him as no intelligible eloquence could have done, and the old man sobbed with a mournfulness not unmingled with satisfaction.

My own remarks were of the same tenor as those of my comrades, and I know that the feelings that prompted them were heartfelt and sincere. We were all sincere, and all deeply moved and earnest, for we were in the presence of death and without hope. I threw away my pipe, and in doing it felt that at last I was free of a hated vice and one that had ridden me like a tyrant all my days. While I yet talked, the thought of the good I might have done in the world and the still greater good I might *now* do, with these new incentives and higher and better aims to guide me if I could only be spared a few years longer, overcame me and the tears came again. We put our arms about each other's necks and awaited the warning drowsiness that precedes death by freezing.

It came stealing over us presently, and then we bade each other a last farewell. A delicious dreaminess wrought its web about my yielding senses, while the snow-flakes wove a winding sheet about my conquered body. Oblivion came. The battle of life was done.

Chapter XXXIII

I do not know how long I was in a state of forgetfulness, but it seemed an age. A vague consciousness grew upon me by degrees, and then came a gathering anguish of pain in my limbs and through all my body. I shuddered. The thought flitted through my brain, "this is death—this is the hereafter."

Then came a white upheaval at my side, and a voice said, with bitterness:

"Will some gentleman be so good as to kick me behind?"

It was Ballou—at least it was a towzled snow image in a sitting posture, with Ballou's voice.

I rose up, and there in the gray dawn, not fifteen steps from us, were the frame buildings of a stage station, and under a shed stood our still saddled and bridled horses!

An arched snow-drift broke up, now, and Ollendorff emerged from it, and the three of us sat and stared at the houses without speaking a word. We really had nothing to say. We were like the profane man who could not "do the subject justice," the whole situation was so painfully ridiculous and humiliating that words were tame and we did not know where to commence anyhow.

The joy in our hearts at our deliverance was poisoned; well-nigh dissipated, indeed. We presently began to grow pettish by degrees, and sullen; and then, angry at each other, angry at ourselves, angry at everything in general, we moodily dusted the snow from our clothing and in unsociable single file plowed our way to the horses, unsaddled them, and sought shelter in the station.

I have scarcely exaggerated a detail of this curious and absurd adventure. It occurred almost exactly as I have stated it. We actually went into camp in a snow-drift in a desert, at midnight in a storm, forlorn and hopeless, within fifteen steps of a comfortable inn.

For two hours we sat apart in the station and ruminated in disgust. The mystery was gone, now, and it was plain enough why the horses had deserted us. Without a doubt they were under that shed a quarter of a minute after they had left us, and they must have overheard and enjoyed all our confessions and lamentations.

After breakfast we felt better, and the zest of life soon came back. The world looked bright again, and existence was as dear to us as ever. Presently an uneasiness came over me—grew upon me—assailed me without ceasing. Alas, my regeneration was not complete—I wanted to smoke! I resisted with all my strength, but the flesh was weak. I wandered away alone and wrestled with myself an hour. I recalled my promises of reform and preached to myself persuasively, upbraidingly, exhaustively. But it was all vain, I shortly found myself sneaking among the snow-drifts hunting for my pipe. I discovered it after a considerable search, and crept away to hide myself and enjoy it. I remained behind the barn a good while, asking myself how I would feel if my braver, stronger, truer comrades should catch me in my degradation. At last I lit the pipe, and no human being can feel meaner and baser than I did then. I was ashamed of being in my own pitiful company. Still dreading discovery, I felt that perhaps the further side of the barn would be somewhat safer, and so I turned the corner. As I turned the one corner, smoking, Ollendorff turned the other with his bottle to his lips, and between us sat unconscious Ballou deep in a game of "solitaire" with the old greasy cards!

Absurdity could go no farther. We shook hands and agreed to say no more about "reform" and "examples to the rising generation."

Charles Dudley Warner

"Sixth Week" in *My Summer in a Garden*

What I Know about Gardening

Somebody has sent me a new sort of hoe, with the wish that I should speak favorably of it, if I can consistently. I willingly do so, but with the understanding that I am to be at liberty to speak just as courteously of any other hoe which I may receive. If I understand religious morals, this is the position of the religious press with regard to bitters and wringing-machines. In some cases, the responsibility of such a recommendation is shifted upon the wife of the editor or clergyman. Polly says she is entirely willing to make a certificate, accompanied with an affidavit, with regard to this hoe; but her habit of sitting about the garden-walk, on an inverted flower-pot, while I hoe, somewhat destroys the practical value of her testimony.

As to this hoe, I do not mind saying that it has changed my view of the desirableness and value of human life. It has, in fact, made life a holiday to me. It is made on the principle that man is an upright, sensible, reasonable being, and not a grovelling wretch. It does away with the necessity of the hinge in the back. The handle is seven and a half feet long. There are two narrow blades, sharp on both edges, which come together at an obtuse angle in front; and as you walk along with this hoe before you, pushing and pulling with a gentle motion, the weeds fall at every thrust and withdrawal, and the slaughter is immediate and wide-spread. When I got this hoe I was troubled with sleepless mornings, pains in the back, kleptomania with regard to new weeders; when I went into my garden I was always sure to see something. In this disordered state of mind and body I got this hoe. The morning after a day of using it I slept perfectly and late. I regained my respect for the eighth commandment. After two doses of the hoe in the garden, the weeds entirely disappeared. Trying it a third morning, I was obliged to throw it over the fence in order to save from destruction the green things that ought to grow in the garden. Of course, this is figurative language. What I mean is, that the fascination of using this hoe is such that you are sorely tempted to employ it upon your vegetables, after the weeds are laid low, and must hastily withdraw it, to avoid unpleasant results. I make this explanation, because I intend to put nothing into these agricultural papers that will not bear the strictest scientific investigation; nothing that the youngest child cannot understand and cry for; nothing that the oldest and wisest men will not need to study with care.

I need not add that the care of a garden with this hoe becomes the merest pastime. I would not be without one for a single night. The only danger is, that you may rather make an idol of the hoe, and somewhat neglect your garden in explaining it, and fooling about with it. I almost think that, with one of these in the hands of an ordinary day-laborer, you might see at nightwhere he had been working.

Let us have peas. I have been a zealous advocate of the birds. I have rejoiced in their multiplication.

I have endured their concerts at four o'clock in the morning without a murmur. Let them come, I said, and eat the worms, in order that we, later, may enjoy the foliage and the fruits of the earth. We have a cat, a magnificent animal, of the sex which votes (but not a pole-cat),—so large and powerful that, if he were in the army, he would be called Long Tom. He is a cat of fine disposition, the most irreproachable morals I ever saw thrown away in a cat, and a splendid hunter. He spends his nights, not in social dissipation, but in gathering in rats, mice, flying-squirrels, and also birds. When he first brought me a bird, I told him that it was wrong, and tried to convince him, while he was eating it, that he was doing wrong; for he is a reasonable cat, and understands pretty much everything except the binomial theorem and the time down the cycloidal arc. But with no effect. The killing of birds went on to my great regret and shame.

The other day I went to my garden to get a mess of peas. I had seen, the day before, that they were just ready to pick. How I had lined the ground, planted, hoed, bushed them! The bushes were very fine,—seven feet high, and of good wood. How I had delighted in the growing, the blowing, the podding! What a touching thought it was that they had all podded for me! When I went to pick them, I found the pods all split open, and the peas gone. The dear little birds, who are so fond of the strawberries, had eaten them all. Perhaps there were left as many as I planted: I did not count them. I made a rapid estimate of the cost of the seed, the interest of the ground, the price of labor, the value of the bushes, the anxiety of weeks of watchfulness. I looked about me on the face of Nature. The wind blew from the south so soft and treacherous! A thrush sang in the woods so deceitfully! All Nature seemed fair. But who was to give me back my peas? The fowls of the air have peas; but what has man?

I went into the house. I called Calvin. (That is the name of our cat, given him on account of his gravity, morality, and uprightness. We never familiarly call him John.) I petted Calvin. I lavished upon him an enthusiastic fondness. I told him that he had no fault; that the one action that I had called a vice was an heroic exhibition of regard for my interests. I bade him go and do likewise continually. I now saw how much better instinct is than mere unguided reason. Calvin knew. If he had put his opinion into English (instead of his native catalogue), it would have been: "You need not teach your grandmother to suck eggs." It was only the round of Nature. The worms eat a noxious something in the ground. The birds eat the worms. Calvin eats the birds. We eat—no we do not eat Calvin. There the chain stops. When you ascend the scale of being, and come to an animal that is, like ourselves, inedible, you have arrived at a result where you can rest. Let us respect the cat. He completes an edible chain.

I have little heart to discuss methods of raising peas. It occurs to me that I can have an iron pea-bush, a sort of trellis, through which I could discharge electricity at frequent intervals, and electrify the birds to death when they alight: for they stand upon my beautiful brush in order to pick out the peas. An apparatus of this kind, with an operator, would cost, however, about as much as the peas. A neighbor suggests that I might put up a scarecrow near the vines, which would keep the birds away. I am doubtful about it: the birds are too much accustomed to seeing a person in poor clothes in the garden to care much for that. Another neighbor suggests that the birds do not open the pods; that a sort of blast, apt to come after rain, splits the pods, and the birds then eat the peas. It may be so. There seems to be complete unity of action between the blast and the birds. But, good neighbors, kind friends, I desire that you will not increase, by talk, a disappointment which you cannot assuage.

About the Editor

A resident of Helena, Montana, since 1989, Amy Kelley grew up in a family of five girls in Madison, Wisconsin, where summer days were spent at the neighborhood pool and family vacations were spent camping. Rather than a serene wilderness experience, Amy recalls camping as a rowdy family affair, where telling stories around the campfire played an important role.

Since graduating from Oberlin College in 1983, Amy has worked primarily for various public interest organizations as an organizer, writer, publications designer, lobbyist, advocate, and illustrator. Her work experience has taken some interesting side jogs as well, including two seasons working at a fly-fishing lodge in southern Chile.

This anthology series was compiled over two years, during which time Amy left Helena to attend art school in Portland, Oregon. Now back in Helena, her freelance work life affords ample opportunity to take off into the mountains and Montana's open spaces for mountain biking, hiking, camping, and cross-country skiing.

An Ornery Bunch

Tales and Anecdotes Collected by the WPA Montana Writers' Project 1935–1942

This TwoDot* book presents the best of the Montana WPA folklore collection.

ISBN 1-56044-842-3   **$14.95**

* TwoDot is an imprint of Falcon® Publishing, Inc.

condensed from HORSE TRADING

Big Gus Thompson was a horse trader pure but not simple. One day Gus was sitting on the porch of the Irma Hotel when a well-dressed dude came up.

"Mr. Thompson," said he, "I've heard you're one of the best judges of horse flesh and that you're a man who really knows horses and your judgment is to be trusted."

"Well, that's a mighty nice compliment. What can I do for you?"

"I'd like a gentle horse I can trust with my daughter, but I want a good one and a fast one."

"I've got just the horse you want. It's a mighty fine animal and fills your requirements— gentle but fast." He turned to his son Ted. "Bring out that sprint horse I got the other day."

The horse was a beauty, gentle but spirited and pranced proudly up and down.

"That's just the horse I want," declared the dude.

"Well," said Thompson, "you shouldn't buy a horse right off the bat like that. I don't want to sell him until you see what he can do. Ted, saddle 'im up."

In a few minutes Ted Thompson was back again with the horse saddled and bridled. He raced the animal up and down the main street and the horse fairly flew. The dude reached for his wallet and pulled out $200. "I'll take him right now."

A few days later Thompson was again on the porch of the hotel and again the dude appeared.

"Mr. Thompson, do you remember that horse I bought from you a few days ago?"

"You bet I do," drawled Thompson. "A mighty fine animal."

"Mr. Thompson, did you know that horse was twenty-three years old?"

"Why, yes, I do remember something about that."

"And, Mr. Thompson, did you know that horse was totally blind in one eye and can barely see out of the other?"

"Why, yes, I did know about that."

The dude transfixed Thompson with a stern, hard glare. "Then, why," he asked coldly, "didn't you tell me about those things?"

Thompson leaned forward confidentially in his chair. "You see, Mister," he confided, "I bought that horse a short time ago from Bear Paw, down on the Crow Reservation. Bear Paw didn't tell me anything about that and so naturally I thought it was a secret."